Just why was Madame Defarge so keen to kill every member of the Marquis D'Evrémonde's family? The answer is here, in Charles Dickens' classic story of plot and intrigue, which paints a vivid picture of the people involved in the French Revolution: their fear, bitterness, joy, and, at last, triumph.

First edition

© LADYBIRD BOOKS LTD MCMLXXXI

A TALE OF TWO CITIES

by Charles Dickens

retold in simple language
by Joan Collins

with illustrations by Frank Humphris

Ladybird Books Loughborough

A Tale of Two Cities

It was a foggy November night in the year 1775. Weary horses were struggling up Shooter's Hill, dragging the heavy Dover mail-coach. Up on the box, the coachman, armed with a blunderbuss, was on the lookout for highwaymen. He could hardly see a yard ahead. The passengers had got down, to reduce the load, and were squelching along in the mud, in their jackboots.

Suddenly, out of the mist, a rider came galloping.

'Stand! Or I'll fire!' cried the coachman.

'I want a passenger!'

'What passenger?'

'Mr Jarvis Lorry, the banker.'

One of the passengers said, shakily: 'What is it, Jerry?' He turned to the coachman. 'It's all right, I know this man.'

The coachman lowered his blunderbuss, and the passengers scrambled to get their watches and their money out of their boots, where they had hidden them in fright.

Jerry handed Mr Lorry a paper. It read: 'Wait at Dover for Mam'selle.'

Mr Lorry replied, mysteriously: 'Say my answer is "RECALLED TO LIFE".'

'That's a blazing strange answer,' said Jerry, hoarsely.

And so it was, as we shall see.

5

At Dover, in the gloomy inn-parlour, by the light of two tall candles, Mr Lorry met 'Mam'selle', a beautiful seventeen year old girl, with golden hair and puzzled blue eyes.

She was Lucie Manette, the daughter of an old business friend; he had brought her to England from France as a baby. She believed herself an orphan.

Now Mr Lorry had to tell her that her father was still alive. He had been locked up in the dreaded Bastille prison in Paris for eighteen years, and no one had been able to trace him. Now at last he had been found, and was free.

'He has been found. Greatly changed. Almost a wreck. We will go to him in Paris, and you must restore him to life.'

Lucie looked wonderingly at this precise old gentleman, in his neat brown suit and tidy wig, who had brought her such astounding news. She was pale with shock, and shivering.

'I am going to see his ghost! It will be his ghost, not him,' she said piteously.

Mr Lorry had to go to Paris on business for the bank. He and Lucie found their way, however, to a miserably poor part of the city. The winding streets smelled horrible, and ragged, hungry people lurked like wild animals in the alleyways. There was hardly any food in the shops.

As they passed down the cobbled streets, a wine-barrel fell off a cart and cracked like a walnut-shell. At once the people rushed to scoop up the spilled wine with anything they could find, even their hands, though the ground was muddy. It was like a game, but the wine smeared their mouths with red stains, so that they looked frightening. One tall fellow, in a dirty night-cap, scrawled a word on the wall with his wine-stained finger – BLOOD! There was trouble brewing in this quarter of Paris.

Lucie and Mr Lorry hurried into a wine-shop nearby, which was owned by Monsieur Defarge, a thickset man with a strong face. His wife, Madame Defarge, sat knitting at the counter. Nothing escaped her beady eyes.

'It is not often, Jacques,' said a customer, 'that these miserable beasts have a taste of wine, or anything but black bread – and death.'

'You are right, Jacques,' said another.

Lucie thought it queer they were both called Jacques. It sounded almost like a password. Monsieur Defarge looked angry, as if he could be a dangerous man if roused.

When Monsieur Defarge knew she was the daughter of his old master, he took Lucie up to a secret hiding-place, high up in the rooftops.

There, in a tiny dark garret, sat an old white-haired man, very busy mending shoes. His hollow eyes could not bear more light, and he was in rags and tatters.

Monsieur Defarge asked him his name, and he answered in a faint, creaking voice, as if he had not used it for some time.

'One Hundred and Five, North Tower.' It was his cell number.

After a time, he began to look at Lucie's face and golden hair, as if she reminded him of someone.

'Are you the jailer's daughter?'

'No.'

'Who are you?'

He took out a soiled rag on a string, hanging from his neck. In it were a few threads of golden hair. Tears came into his eyes. They were all he had to remind him of his wife. Mr Lorry remembered she had looked just like Lucie.

Lucie touched him gently.

'I have come to take you home, father, and to look after you.'

They were smuggled out of Paris that night, past the sentries at the gate, by Monsieur Defarge and his friends. As the coach drove off into the darkness, Mr Lorry wondered if Dr Manette would ever regain his memory and his happiness.

Five years later

It was the year 1780, five years had passed. Lucie and her father were living in a quiet street in London, near enough to the country to have a view of fields and trees.

Lucie's father had taken up his old profession; he was a doctor and greatly respected. But he kept the old cobbler's bench and tools in an upstairs room. Sometimes, when the memory of his prison days came back, he could be heard at night, tapping away, mending shoes. Lucie would worry about her father at these times.

Their housekeeper, Miss Pross, was a fierce lady, with a red face and red hair. She guarded Dr Manette and Lucie (whom she called 'Ladybird') from all intruders, especially young men, who were attracted by Lucie's beauty and gentle ways.

Two such young men had met Lucie in a strange way.

Jerry Cruncher, Mr Lorry's servant (he who had stopped the Dover coach five years before), was on another errand for his master. This time it was to the Old Bailey, where Mr Lorry was giving evidence in a trial.

The Old Bailey was the court where traitors and murderers were tried, and it was crowded with sightseers.

'What's on?' Jerry asked the man sitting next to him, in his hoarse voice.

'Nothing yet.'

'What's coming on?'

'They're trying a French traitor.'

'He'll be quartered, then?'

'Ah,' returned the man with relish, 'he'll be drawn on a hurdle to be half-hanged, and then his head will be chopped off, and he'll be cut into quarters. That's the sentence.'

'If he's found Guilty, you mean to say,' added Jerry.

'Oh, they'll find him Guilty! Don't you be afraid of that!'

The prisoner at the bar, a tall young Frenchman, stood there with dignity. He had long dark hair, tied back with a ribbon, and wore plain grey clothes. He was good-looking, sunburnt, with dark eyes. He was accused of being a spy for the French King, and gave his name as Charles Darnay.

On the lawyers' bench sprawled a man with an untidy wig, a torn gown, and his hands in his pockets, staring up at a fly on the ceiling. He had a remarkable likeness to the prisoner. This was Sydney Carton; he had a reckless look, as if he cared for nobody, not even himself.

Mr Lorry, Lucie and Dr Manette had to give evidence because when they returned from France to England, they had travelled on the same boat as the prisoner. Lucie was nearly in tears. She could not believe anything wrong of the kind young man who had befriended them on the voyage. Charles said his trips to England were on family business and he was not a spy. His servant and another man, John Barsad, accused him.

Charles's counsel was cross-examining a witness, when Sydney Carton suddenly flicked him a screwed-up piece of paper. When counsel had read it, he said:

'You say again that you are quite sure it was the prisoner?'

The witness was quite sure.

'Did you ever see anybody like the prisoner?'

Not so like (the witness said) that he could be mistaken.

'Look well at that gentleman, my learned friend there . . .' (pointing at Sydney Carton, who swept off his wig with a bow) '. . . and then at the prisoner. Don't they look like each other?'

The witness had to agree, so Charles Darnay was found 'Not Guilty', thanks to Sydney Carton's quick thinking.

Charles Darnay and Sydney Carton both became welcome visitors at the home of Lucie and Dr Manette. Charles took a post as a French teacher, as he did not want to go back to France. He began to pay court to Lucie, who was already fond of him.

Miss Pross was not so struck by him and could be heard muttering, 'I don't want dozens of people who are not at all worthy of her to come here after Ladybird.'

Dr Manette behaved oddly. He liked and respected Charles, but something was worrying him. At times he would be heard tapping away at his shoe-mending, late at night, a sign that all was not well.

Sydney Carton, too, loved Lucie. But he knew he had nothing to offer her. He almost hated Charles Darnay for being so much like him, and for being what he might have been.

Carton had been a clever lawyer, till he began drinking too much. When he fell in love with Lucie, he bitterly regretted his past life.

He told Lucie his feelings one day, when he realised she would probably marry Charles. She pleaded with him to change his ways and promised always to be his friend.

He looked at her very seriously, and said:

'Think now and then, that there is a man who would give his life to save somebody you loved.' Lucie did not understand him at that time.

The storm gathers in France

In France, the aristocrats did not believe the poor would ever rise against them. They treated the peasants as if they had no human feelings.

One of the worst of these callous nobles was the Marquis D'Evrémonde. He was finely dressed and haughty, with a pale mask of a face. His coach went at such a speed in the country that the common people had to

scramble out of its way. He never told the coachman to take care.

One day he went too far. The horses ran over a baby and dragged it in the dust. Angry men and women stopped the coach.

'What has gone wrong?' asked the Marquis calmly, looking out.

A tall man in a nightcap had caught up a bundle from the horses' feet, and was down in the mud, howling over it like a wild animal.

'Why does he make that abominable noise? Is it his child? You people should take better care of yourselves and your children. You are always getting in the way. How do I know what injury you have done my horses? See – give him that!' He threw a gold coin down in the road.

As the coach drove off, something rattled into the coach. It was the coin.

'Who threw that?' cried the Marquis angrily.

That night, the Marquis was found stabbed to death in his bedroom. On the dagger, a label said:

'Drive him fast to his tomb. A present from – Jacques.'

('Jacques' was the secret name the poor people used amongst themselves as a password.)

In the wine-shop in Paris, Madame Defarge
sat knitting as usual behind the counter, while
the customers played cards. A road-mender

from the country came in with the news that the man who had stabbed the Marquis D'Evrémonde had been caught and hanged.

Madame kept a kind of register of such happenings. She cleverly knitted the names of those responsible into her pattern. One day, the English spy, John Barsad, who had given evidence at the Old Bailey, came to the wine-shop. He asked her about her knitting.

'You knit with great skill, Madame.'

'I am used to it.'

'May one ask what it is for?'

'Just to pass the time,' said Madame, while her fingers moved nimbly.

'Not for use?'

'I may find a use for it some day,' said Madame, grimly.

When her husband came in, John Barsad told him about Dr Manette's daughter, Lucie, who was going to marry Charles Darnay. Charles was the nephew of the Marquis D'Evrémonde.

When Madame Defarge heard that, her fingers moved again. She was knitting Charles Darnay's name into her work. Then she rolled up her knitting and put it carefully away.

Charles and Lucie were planning their wedding. Charles had heard that his uncle, who was his secret enemy, had been murdered, so Charles was now the new Marquis D'Evrémonde. He had hated his uncle's cruelty and was sorry for the peasants. He wrote to his steward, Gabelle, telling him not to charge the peasants any rent. The only person he told about his new title was Dr Manette, and he still called himself Charles Darnay.

Sydney Carton got over his jealousy of Charles and wanted to be a true friend of the family. Charles told Lucie this, and she said how sorry she was for Sydney.

'He has a good heart, but he seldom shows his feelings.'

After the wedding, Dr Manette had one of his bad turns, remembering the prison. He took to his shoe-mending again. But he gradually recovered and, in the years that followed, he lived happily with Lucie, Charles and their family, until something happened which was to change all their lives.

The storm breaks

By 1792, the beautiful countryside of France was suffering from a famine. The corn harvest had failed. Bread was so dear and so scarce that even if the poor had had money, they could not have bought it. Instead, they were cooking up messes of leaves, grass and onion scrapings to eat. They were so poor because of the heavy taxes they had to pay to the State, to the Church and also to the lord, who made them work on his land for nothing. In the towns it was just as bad. There was no work, no trade and no food.

The aristocrats and the clergy paid no taxes. Everybody else had to pay to keep up the nobles' great houses, their hundreds of servants, and their fine clothes, which looked as if a never-ending fancy dress party was going on. Sooner or later revolution was going to break out, for the poor people were hungry and angry, and nothing was being done to help them. The nobles had rights of life and death over the poor and all who opposed them were hanged, or imprisoned for life, in places like the Bastille.

In the slums of Paris the people were maddened by these wrongs and their tempers were at fever-heat. A tremendous roar went up in the streets, and a forest of ragged arms, like shrivelled branches, waved in the air, clutching any weapons they could find — knives, bars of iron, wood, axes and even stones from the walls.

Like a whirlpool, the crowd surged around the wine-shop, which was the centre of activity. Defarge was issuing orders to Jacques One, Two and Three. Madame Defarge was holding an axe instead of her knitting.

'Citizens and friends, we are ready!' cried Defarge in his strong voice. 'To the Bastille!'

The crowd swept with a great roar to the hated prison, and the attack began. Fire and smoke were belching forth, bells ringing and drums beating. There were now five and twenty thousand Jacques, all hurling themselves into the attack, led by Defarge and his wife, who cried:

'To me, women! We can kill as well as the men when the place is taken!'

For four fierce hours the great sea of vengeance beat against the walls of the prison, till at last a white flag of surrender was seen, and the tide of attackers swept Defarge over the drawbridge and into the Bastille itself.

'The prisoners!'

'The records!'

'The secret cells!'

'The instruments of torture!'

But Defarge had one special purpose.

'Show me the North Tower – One Hundred and Five!' A frightened warder took him to what had been Dr Manette's cell. Defarge searched it thoroughly and discovered some papers in a hiding place behind a brick in the chimney.

All this happened on 14th July, 1789.

Mr Lorry, very upset by what was happening there, returned from a business trip to Paris in the autumn of 1792, bringing a letter addressed to the Marquis D'Evrémonde. He showed it to Charles Darnay and asked if he knew the man.

'I can deliver it,' said Charles, without giving away that he was Evrémonde. He opened and read it when he was alone, and cried, 'I must go to France at once!'

The letter was from his steward, Gabelle, who had been thrown into prison. He wanted Charles to go back to help him.

'For the love of heaven, of justice, of generosity, for the honour of your noble name.'

This was a plea Charles could not refuse, and he set off for France that night.

When Charles reached France he found that the King was in prison and that the people were in charge. He could get nowhere without papers to show he was a loyal citizen. Rough guards, wearing red caps, dragged him off to Paris, where the crowds shouted at him, and Citizen Defarge was put in charge of him.

'Where are this prisoner's papers?' asked Defarge. When he saw them, he realised who Charles was. Charles was taken to an officer, who told him he had no rights, as he was an aristocrat, and was to be imprisoned 'in secret'.

Defarge asked him if it was true he had married Dr Manette's daughter. Charles said he had.

'Why on earth have you come back to France to risk the guillotine?'

Charles told him it was to help the steward, and begged him to take a message to Mr Lorry's Paris office.

'I will do nothing for you. My duty is to my country and my people,' was the stern answer.

The prison of La Force was a gloomy place, dark and filthy, with a horrible smell of foul sleep about it. Charles passed through a long room with a low arched ceiling, crowded with prisoners, both men and women. These were

the aristocrats, still well-mannered, proud, and in the rags of their once fine clothes. Charles thought they looked like ghosts — 'They are a company of the dead!' he thought.

He was locked into a cell by himself and refused anything to write with. He knew then he could expect no justice or mercy, and that there was no hope.

Down in the courtyard below Mr Lorry's Paris office, a hideous noise went on. It was the people sharpening their knives and hatchets on a grindstone.

'They are going to murder the prisoners!' thought Mr Lorry, in horror.

Suddenly Lucie and Dr Manette appeared at the door, a little girl with them.

'What has happened? What has brought you here to Paris?'

'My husband!' cried Lucie.

Dr Manette said: 'I have been a Bastille prisoner. No one in Paris would harm me. I have come to help Charles out of danger.'

He went down into the courtyard, and the bloodthirsty mob greeted him with cheers. He called for help for Charles Darnay. They carried him off, excitedly, while Lucie waited, with old Mr Lorry and her little girl, for his return.

In the morning, Defarge came with a message from Dr Manette: 'Charles is safe, but I cannot leave this place yet.' Defarge had brought his wife with him and Lucie kissed her hand in gratitude. It felt cold and heavy.

'Is this his child?' said Madame Defarge, pointing a knitting needle at the little girl as if it were a finger of Fate.

'Do help me!' pleaded Lucie. 'Think of me as a sister and mother.'

'We have seen our sisters and mothers and their children suffer all their lives. One more makes little difference.'

She went away, still knitting, leaving Lucie very troubled. 'That dreadful woman seems to cast a shadow on me and all my hopes,' she thought.

Now Lucie went every day with her little girl to walk outside the prison and look up at Charles's cell window. She was watched by Madame Defarge, who was determined that none of that family should escape the guillotine.

The guillotine (which the people called 'Madame') was the instrument of execution. The aristocrats were taken in carts (called tumbrils) to the place where a tall scaffolding stood. There they had to kneel and place their heads on a block. A sharp axe-blade on a pulley dropped down with a rush on their necks, and

their heads fell into a basket. Madame Defarge and the other women sat knitting around it, counting the heads as they fell.

La Guillotine was a wonderful cure for the headache, they said.

At last Charles was brought to trial before the Citizens' Tribunal. Dr Manette, Mr Lorry and Gabelle gave evidence for him, and the Tribunal was on his side. He was set free and carried shoulder high by the cheering people, back to his lodgings.

Dr Manette gazed happily at the little family. 'I have saved him!' he thought.

But their happiness was not to last long. That night, a heavy blow was struck on the door, and four rough men in red caps, armed with pistols, entered the room.

'The Citizen Evrémonde, called Darnay?'

'Who seeks him?'

'I know you, Evrémonde. I saw you today before the Tribunal. You are again the prisoner of the Republic.'

'But why? How can this happen?'

'You have been denounced by the Citizen and Citizeness Defarge and one other.'

'What other?'

'You will be told that tomorrow. I cannot answer.'

And Charles was dragged off once more, this time to the Conciergerie Prison.

Jerry Cruncher, Mr Lorry's servant, was out on an errand for him when all this was happening. Suddenly he saw a face he knew in the street. He called out: 'I know you! You was the spy what was a witness at the Old Bailey trial – what was you called?'

'Barsad,' another voice struck in. The speaker was Sydney Carton. He stood by Jerry's elbow as casually as he might have stood in the Old Bailey itself.

He went on: 'I saw you, Mr Barsad, coming out of the Conciergerie Prison, an hour or so ago. You have a face to be remembered. I followed you to the wine-shop, and from your conversation I guessed your job. Could you favour me with a few minutes of your time at the offices of Mr Lorry's bank?'

'Is that a threat?' said the spy, turning pale.

Barsad was a turnkey, or warder, at the prison where Charles was locked up, and Carton had thought of a plan to use him. He and Jerry knew something about Barsad's past which Barsad would not like the Tribunal to find out, so he agreed to do what Sydney wanted.

Carton's next move was to warn Mr Lorry that Charles had been arrested again, and to ask after Lucie. For some reason he did not ask to see her.

Instead, he prowled the Paris streets that night till he found a chemist's shop open. There he bought a drug which would put a man to sleep for a long time.

'There is nothing more to do,' he said, glancing at the moon, 'until tomorrow.'

In the morning, he made his way to the Tribunal, where he heard the name of Charles Darnay's third accuser. It was none other than Dr Manette. The Doctor knew nothing about it himself. It was Defarge who had put down his name and produced the papers he had found in the Doctor's cell in the Bastille, revealing who had imprisoned him there. Dr Manette could not deny the papers were in his handwriting.

Those responsible had been the Evrémonde brothers, Charles's father and uncle. Between them, they had caused the deaths of an innocent peasant girl, and her brother who tried to defend her. Dr Manette was the only witness, so the Evrémonde brothers had had him put in the Bastille to keep him quiet. Charles was the only living member of his family, so now he was to be put to death for his family's crime, though he had known nothing of it, and indeed had been only a child at the time.

At last Charles understood Dr Manette's distress, when he had learned Charles was an Evrémonde, at the time of the wedding. Madame Defarge's hatred was explained, too. The dead girl and boy were her own sister and brother.

'I have no hope,' said Mr Lorry to Sydney. 'He will perish.'

'Yes, he will perish,' said Sydney. 'There is no real hope.' And he walked very purposefully down the steps.

When Carton returned to Mr Lorry's office, he found Dr Manette was missing. Then they heard his step on the stairs. When he came in, they knew the poor man had lost his memory again.

'I cannot find it and I must have it! Where is it?' He meant his cobbler's bench, which was the only thing that had kept him sane in the dreadful prison.

'He cannot help us now,' said Carton. 'He had better be taken to Lucie. But listen to me and do as I say. I have a good reason.'

They searched for Dr Manette's certificate of permission to leave Paris with his daughter, and found it. Sydney had one, too, which he gave to Mr Lorry, to keep safely for him.

'I am going to visit Charles in prison tonight and I don't want to risk taking it with me, in case I lose it.'

'Do you think Lucie and the child are in danger, too?'

'Yes, from Madame Defarge. You must be ready to leave at two o'clock tomorrow. Persuade them to go with you. Tell Lucie it is Charles's wish. Wait for me, and the moment I come, drive away.'

Charles Darnay was passing his last night in prison, writing a farewell letter to his wife. The next day fifty two heads were to fall and his was to be one of them. He listened to the clock striking the hours. Suddenly his cell door opened, and there was Sydney Carton, a smile on his face and a finger to his lips.

'I bring a message from your wife. Do exactly as I tell you. I have no time to waste.'

He made Charles change clothes with him,

take the ribbon off his hair, and shake it loose, like Carton's. Then he asked him to write a letter to Lucie, at Sydney's dictation. It read: 'You remember some words of mine. You will understand when you see this. I am thankful the time has come when I can prove them.'

As he wrote, Carton put a handkerchief to Charles's face, soaked in the drug he had bought. Charles fell unconscious to the floor, and with the help of Barsad, who had let Carton into the prison, he was smuggled out, leaving Carton in his place.

At the gates of Paris, the guards inspect the coach in which Mr Lorry, Lucie and the family are departing. They joke about Sydney Carton (really Charles Darnay), lying in a drunken stupor in a corner of the carriage.

'We may go now?'

'You may go! Bon voyage!'

In the prison a little servant girl begs Charles Darnay, as she thinks him to be, to hold her hand when they go to the guillotine. Sydney Carton agrees.

Along the Paris streets the death-carts
rumble, hollow and harsh.

'Which is Charles Evrémonde?'

'There, with his hand in the girl's.'

'Down with Evrémonde! To the guillotine,
aristo!'

The clocks strike three. There is La Guillotine. In front of it are rows of women, knitting.

The first tumbril empties. Crash! A head is held up. The women never stop knitting, as one by one they count the heads.

'Keep your eye on me, child. Look at nothing else.'

'I do not mind if I hold your hand, but will they be quick?'

'They will be quick. Don't be afraid.'

She goes before him — is gone. The knitting women count Twenty Two.

Sydney saw in his mind Lucie and her family, going safely to England. He thought: 'It is a far, far, better thing I do than I have ever done. It is a far, far, better rest I go to than I have ever known.'

The murmuring of many voices, the upturning of many faces, all flash away. Twenty Three.

They said of him afterwards that his was the peacefullest face they had ever seen.

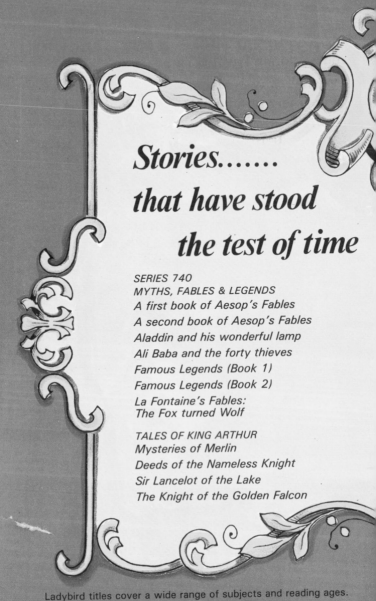

Stories.......
that have stood
the test of time

Ladybird titles cover a wide range of subjects and reading ages.
Write for a free illustrated list from the publishers:
LADYBIRD BOOKS LTD Loughborough Leicestershire England